Harvest Fever

Jeffery Martin
Botzenhart

Publisher's Note:

This is a work of fiction. All names, characters, places, and events are the work of the author's imagination.

Any resemblance to real persons, places, or events is coincidental.

Solstice Publishing - www.solsticepublishing.com

Harvest Fever
By
Jeffery Martin Botzenhart

Dedication

A special thanks to my mom for letting me
watch all those old science-fiction movies
when I was growing up.

Chapter One

After hoisting the last bale of hay up to the loft, Orrville sat down, exhausted, looking out at the brilliantly colored late afternoon streaked orange sky. Soaked with sweat from laboring for hours in the unseasonably warm temperatures nearing ninety degrees, he was happy the workday had come to an end. But this relief was fleeting, knowing what would come next, he heard a man call out his name. He dragged himself up and climbed down the ladder near the barn loft opening. "Yes, Mister Verner?"

"Here's your pay for a hard week's work, Son," the farm's owner said as he handed Orrville fifty dollars. "Now you make sure to keep this away from your stepdaddy, you hear?"

"Yes, Sir," Orrville responded as he took the money and glanced away in embarrassment. It seemed everyone in and around Birchwood Hollow, Tennessee knew of his stepdad's gambling addiction, and all the money he'd lost over time. Many guessed the truth that he'd spent and stolen almost all the hard-earned savings Orrville and his late mom had. And while most of these same people believed Orrville should have been removed from his stepdad's care, no one actually stepped forward to help with this. But what with his eighteenth birthday only days away, Orrville hoped to endure these last few days with him before leaving to find his own place, maybe somewhere far away.

Collecting his empty water jug and shirt, Orrville waved good evening to Mister Verner and his wife and began walking the mile home. He treaded a path down the wooded lane, taking his time to appreciate the autumn-colored leaves clinging to the branches. Stray gusts of warm wind caused the overhead tree canopy to shiver, sending a few leaves in a flurry gliding down to the ground to decay with the others already fallen. Orrville remembered his mom loving this time of year and understood why. Though they couldn't afford a casket or plot in the local cemetery after she died of cancer, he made certain to spread her ashes across her favorite secluded knoll in the woods, one surrounded by large trees appearing on fire when graced with crimson, orange, and gold shades each October.

Thinking of her, it was hard to believe two years had gone by since she died. So far, they were two of the worst years of his life, not counting the three bad years before this when she'd married Henry Lee Huston. Many times he asked her why she married him and each time she answered the same, claiming to love him. Orrville knew the truth though. With his mom having lost her job as a telemarketer when the center moved away, they had very little money left to live off.

Having never known his birth dad, it was just the two of them until Henry Lee showed up one day, charming her with his fake smile. Out of love and respect for his mom, Orrville never challenged her decision to marry Henry Lee. But after the first time he beat her and stole what little money she'd saved, Orrville's distrust of his stepdad grew to a simmering hatred. It proved pointless though, pleading with her to escape from him, as she wouldn't consider it.

After his mom died, he thought of running away. Yet out here in the depths of Appalachia there were too few places to run away to. Besides lacking enough money to travel far on a bus, he believed his stepdad would find him and bring him home. Considering the town's sheriff is one of Henry Lee's gambling buddies, he knew the law wouldn't offer him with any help either. Once when Henry Lee had whipped him for coming home late, Orrville sought Sheriff Connolly's help. But the sheriff turned a blind eye to the deep welts on Orrville's back, instead telling him to be a good boy so things like that don't happen again.

With their small backwoods trailer too soon coming into view, Orrville imagined what he'd find when he stepped inside. It was always the same. Littered everywhere would be empty or near empty bottles of alcohol, ashes from cigarettes all over the furniture, and heaps of trash and dirty dishes covering the kitchen counters. Before going to bed each night Orrville made sure to clean the mess up, but it would appear again the next day and the day after that and so on. Maybe this would be his last week, though, of being his stepdad's personal housekeeper.

Walking up to the front door, Orrville stopped and inhaled a deep breath for courage before going inside. Swallowing hard, he silently counted to ten and then grabbed the door handle. But as soon as he walked inside, his jaw dropped when he saw what was waiting there for him.

Everything in sight was neat and clean, including Henry Lee. Usually wearing a stained faded white muscle shirt and torn soiled jeans, tonight his stepdad stood there dressed in a nice button-down blue and black plaid shirt and black cargo pants. Clean shaven with his hair combed, Henry Lee looked like he was heading to church, which he never did.

As for the small living room, no traces of cigarette ashes or empty bottles of alcohol could be found. Not since his mom was alive had he seen the living room and kitchen so spotless when not cleaned up by him. There was even food cooking on the stove. Clearly understanding his shock, Henry Lee remarked, "I know it's only canned stew—but I don't really know much about cooking."

Though still stunned by what he was seeing, Orrville forced out, "I'm sure it will taste just fine. It smells good."

"Don't take this wrong," Henry Lee continued, "But—you stink like the Verner's farm. You got time before the stew is hot. Why don't you go take a shower?"

Nodding his head, Orrville passed by his stepdad on his way to his bedroom. Closing the door behind him, he pressed his ear against the wood surface wanting to make sure Henry Lee hadn't followed him. Hearing nothing from the other side, Orrville tugged his fifty dollars pay from his pocket and knelt down. Running his fingers across the wood floor, he found his secret loose board and pulled it up. Adding his money to the one hundred and fifty-three dollars hidden within the pages of a small book of poems his mom gave him, Orrville then replaced the board and stood up. Again pressing his ear to the door he still heard no sounds from the other side.

Kicking off his boots and stripping off his jeans, he wrapped a towel around his waist before heading to the bathroom. Once in the shower, the warm water soothed over his tired sore muscles. For a few minutes, he just stood there before lathering with soap. After he finished cleaning the dirt and sweat off his skin, he wiped the fog off the mirror and combed his short brown hair. He remembered his mom telling him how handsome she thought he was and wondered if he looked anything like his birth dad. Orrville was happy his muscular frame appeared nothing like Henry Lee's slightly overweight body. He never wanted anyone to mistakenly think that he and his stepdad were blood related.

Returning to his room and pulling on a fresh pair of jeans, Orrville padded barefoot out to the kitchen. "Supper's ready," Henry Lee said as he placed two bowls of stew down on the table. A glass of milk and an apple were also set there for Orrville.

"Thanks," he offered to his stepdad as they sat down to eat. Orrville couldn't recall sharing a moment like this with Henry Lee, leaving him slightly relieved—but also concerned. Though a part of him regretted thinking this, Orrville wondered why Henry Lee was acting this way. *What's really going on here?* He thought.

Hearing a siren blaring in the distance, they both looked at each other. "That doesn't sound right," Henry Lee said. "The pitch is too high." Orrville just shrugged his shoulders, not really caring about the noise.

"So...how was work on the farm today?" Henry Lee asked, noticeably struggling to make light conversation, something they never did.

"It was fine," Orrville quietly responded. "Kurt didn't show up—so I had to do everything by myself. I'm pretty tired."

"You look beat," Henry Lee commented before taking a bite of his stew. "So...where was Kurt?"

"I don't know. Mister Verner didn't say."

"Well, it's a good thing for Mister Verner that you're a responsible boy." Shocked when hearing this compliment, Orrville just shrugged his shoulders, not knowing how to respond.

"I think the pretty girls in town are gonna like your muscles and that tan you got goin' there."

Again feeling awkward by Henry Lee's remarks, Orrville kept quiet as he ate his dinner.

"We could watch some TV together after I wash the dishes," Henry Lee suggested. "The reception's not too great on that old piece of junk—but if I adjust the antenna, we should be able to watch something."

"I think I'm just gonna go to bed. I'm too tired."

"Yeah, sure."

Feeling his eyelids growing heavy as he finished eating his apple, Orrville rubbed his eyes. "Go on to bed," Henry Lee urged. "I'll take care of the dishes. I'll make you some breakfast tomorrow morning before you head to school." Knowing tomorrow was Sunday he decided not to bother correcting him, figuring he would realize his mistake when he heard the church bells echoing through the valley in the morning.

"Thanks," Orrville uttered, beginning to think his real stepdad had been abducted by kind aliens who left this nice one in his place. "Good night," he said to Henry Lee before heading to his room. Once inside, he closed and locked the door.

Too tired to pull off his jeans, instead he crawled under a patchwork quilt his mom had sewn and closed his eyes.

***

Awakened by movements next to his bed, Orrville opened his eyes a sliver and looked at the time on his clock, showing just a few minutes before eleven. Hearing Henry Lee faintly mumble, "*Damn*", under his breath after kicking something, he knew his stepdad had somehow unlocked his door and was now inside the room with him. It didn't take a lot of thought in guessing he was searching for money. That must have been why he'd been so nice tonight. But Orrville also knew if Henry Lee didn't find what Mister Verner paid him, things could get real bad. Keeping still, continuing to fake sleep, Orrville waited for what would come next.

Sensing weight pressing down on the bed next to him, breathing in the stench of alcohol Orrville again understood how the old Henry Lee had returned. But what happened next proved nothing like any other time before. Orrville's heart nearly stopped beating when feeling Henry Lee's beer gut resting against his bare back. His breathing grew shallow as Henry Lee's fingers traced down his torso to his jeans. Prying the pocket open, Orrville could feel his stepdad searching for money. Then quickly shifted on top of him before he could react, Henry Lee gagged Orrville with his large hand covering his mouth while forcing his struggling arms down by his heavy weight. "Where the hell is the money," Henry Lee rasped.

Fighting to free his pinned body, thrusting his leg up Orrville kneed his stepdad in the groin. Howling in pain, Henry Lee fell off the side of the bed, banging his skull against the dresser. Motionless after he fell to the floor, Orrville fearfully glance down, thinking Henry Lee had been knocked unconscious.

Scrambling out of bed, Orrville forced the loose floorboard up to collect the book of poems with his money hidden inside. He then grabbed his boots and a gray zip-up hoodie and bolted out of this bedroom. Rushing outside, he noticed how his breath fogged and vanished in the chilled midnight air. The grass under his bare feet sent chills coursing through his body as he forced on his boots. Orrville pulled on his hoodie but before zipping it up he froze when blinding lights flooded through the trees from the edge of the woods. Their brilliant beams caused the mist clinging to the ground to look like a glowing, hovering ghost. Orrville spotted shadowed movements rapidly passing in the lights but heard no sounds. Turning, he ran away in the opposite direction. Deeper and deeper he trudged through the thick brush. Stumbling in the pitch blackness, he pressed through the low pine branches. His face, neck, and chest scratched and stinging, he soon found his way to the covered bridge leading out of town. He scooted under the bridge, wedging his trembling body into a sloped spot, watching the flashing lights overhead corrupting the dark night sky. Pulling his knees up to his chest, his body shivered in the near freezing air, listening to the splashing sounds of the rushing river below.

Chapter Two

Startled by his body shuddering after barely falling asleep, Orrville lost his footing and skidded down the slope under the bridge. With nothing to grab hold of, he ended up sliding into the frigid water feet first. His pulse raced as he expelled his last breath before becoming fully submerged, His vision clouded in the murky depths. When he broke the surface, he coughed out water, gasping for air, as he looked fearfully into the surrounding dense fog. He swam over to the riverbank until he was able to stand in the shallow part. Trudging slowly over to the shore, his arms quaked with the effort as he tried to pull himself out of the rushing current. The morning dew soaked grass chilled his fingers as he crawled to his feet.

Orrville was weighted down by the heaviness of his soaked clothes. He thought of taking off his hoodie but stopped when he felt a lump in his pocket. Reaching in, he pulled out the old book of poems. Filled with sadness at how the pages were damaged from being in the water, he opened the soggy cover, which disintegrated in his hand. The ink of much of the printed words had smudged, leaving every word unreadable. Though he wanted to keep the book, the only thing he had left from his mom, now it seemed pointless as it continued to fall apart. Pulling the money hidden inside, he stuffed the bills into his hoodie pocket and then tossed the ruined poems into the river. For a moment, he watched the book float until it submerged just under the surface, disappearing forever.

Climbing up to the covered bridge, he stepped to the side of the road and glanced in both directions. But this being Sunday, he thought the church bells should be ringing by now. They always sounded out a dawn for first mass. By the dim sunlight piercing through the billowing fog, he guessed it was early morning. Orrville wondered if he just hadn't paid attention, hadn't heard them. Either way, the road was too quiet for a Sunday morning in Birchwood Hollow.

Conflicted, Orrville knew he couldn't return home or seek out the sheriff to explain what happened. And with the bus stop in the center of town, escaping from here that way would draw unwanted attention. What if Henry Lee was searching for him? He'd make sure the bus stop was being watched. With the closest towns roughly three miles away in both directions, the best way to reach them was by road.

Any attempt to walk through the thick woods might leave him hopelessly lost in the mountains.

Maybe one of his friends could help him, he sarcastically thought, treated as an outcast by the kids in school because of being poor. He understood the irony of this, considering most of the residents in town were thought of as white trash by people outside the valley. Birchwood Hollow had three classes of people, poor, poorer, and poorest. Everyone knew their standing in the community, with most keeping to their own groups until Sunday when all were accepted as equals in the house of God. Thinking of Pastor McKinnon who was always kind to all, Orrville decided to seek him out, maybe he could help?

The fog grew thicker as he crossed the covered bridge. The eerie silence tainting the heavy air yielded no noticeable sounds with exception of his boots scraping against the wood planks. Reaching the middle point of the bridge, Orrville looked nervously behind him for any traces of headlights. Seeing none, he continued on, breathing a sigh of relief when he reached the other side of the bridge leading toward the town center.

Veiled by the dense fog, the first few houses faintly appeared. Both looked abandoned, offering no traces of people ever having lived inside. Shifting his eyes in each direction, Orrville's breathing grew rapid with each step. His soaked body was chilled. Pressing his palm to his chest, he trembled as he felt his heart nearly bursting through his skin. So many times before he'd been frightened by storms or Henry Lee or even ridiculous stories told of Bigfoot lurking in the woods. But Orrville knew he'd never been scared like this in the past. Church, however, was the one place he always felt safe. If Pastor McKinnon refused to help him escape from this town, Orrville wasn't sure what he would do.

Reaching the bus stop, Orrville halted dead in his tracks. With the rolling fog shrouding the surrounding buildings like smoke billowing from a fire, the thought crossed his mind that somehow he'd arrived in a ghost town. Seeing and hearing no signs of life from anywhere around, he wondered where everyone could be. Certainly, they weren't all in church. The town had just as many sinners as God-fearing Baptists. One or two heathens must be awake in one of these houses.

Resting for a minute on a sidewalk bench, Orrville sat in silence while listening for the echoing sounds of barking dogs. Knowing they never stayed this quiet, he thought of making a loud noise to coax one into barking. Although this might draw attention to him, his growing feelings of dread might subside if he heard at least one local mutt start howling. Cupping his hands around his mouth, Orrville shouted, "Hey!" After the resounding echoes of his voice faded, the unsettling silence returned. "What is going on?" Orrville mumbled under his breath.

Orrville watched for signs of people peeking out from behind the curtains of their darkened windows as he walked down the street toward the church. Though scared, everything seemed more like a strange dream than a nightmare that he couldn't wake up from. He wondered if he *was* in fact dreaming. Maybe his mind decided to play tricks on him? Or maybe he bumped his head like Dorothy in *The Wizard of Oz*? Whatever was going on here, he hoped to at least find the pastor in the church at the top of the hill.

Thinking back to last night, Orrville realized he hadn't given much thought to all those bright lights and shadows outside their trailer. It wasn't uncommon for a group of hunters to go out in the woods after dark for some night shooting, *stupid*…but not uncommon. Most would end up drunk before sunrise, having shot at only each other instead of the deer or wild turkeys they set out to hunt. But he'd never seen beaming lights like that before. What could they have been tracking that they would need such bright lights? Certainly, the lights would scare all the animals away. But then Orrville thought that maybe it *wasn't* hunters. Maybe a prisoner escaped from the nearest penitentiary? The police could have been using floodlights to flush him out of the woods. If they were looking for someone to take to prison, Henry Lee could be their man. For all the abuse and theft he'd committed, he deserved to rot in a cell.

With the fog less intense as he reached the church, Orrville saw no cars or trucks parked close by. Something definitely had happened to keep the faithful from attending Sunday morning mass. Feeling his heart wedged in his throat Orrville climbed the steps and cautiously entered through the main doors. Breathing in the incense tainted air with an oak fragrance from the woodwork he slowly walked past the many rows of pews to the pulpit. The subtle light shafts beaming through the colorful stain glass windows revealed a veil of dust hanging in the air. Seeing none of the candles on the altar lit, he guessed Pastor McKinnon hadn't even stepped inside the sanctuary this morning.

Shaken by the sudden echoing clatter of the doors opening, Orrville fearfully swallowed hard before turning around. When he saw Pastor McKinnon standing there in the doorway, his breath rushed from his lungs along with the release of some of his anxiety. "Where is everyone?" Orrville asked as the pastor came up to him.

"Sit, my son," Pastor McKinnon urged. Taking a seat next to him, Orrville listened as the pastor quickly uttered, "The time for questions has come and gone, my dear boy. You must listen to me. When out for an evening stroll, I heard a blaring siren and witnessed blinding lights in the night sky. Only the sun is brighter than what I saw. And the lights were moving. I have never supported such nonsense as the existence of space aliens, but I am now a believer. I followed one of the hovering lights to the edge of town and watched as it landed in a clearing near the woods."

Looking around, fearful of being watched, both his eyes and expression displayed panic as Pastor McKinnon continued, "Large shadows appeared through the bright lights. I hid from them and then followed them back here to town. Listen, my son. Everyone they found, every man, woman, and child, they took with them. It was as if they had hypnotized them.

Everyone followed the shadows in silence, not one soul resisting."

"This is crazy," Orrville mumbled under his breath.

"I know how all this sounds—but every word is the truth. I would swear on the Bible."

"Is there anyone else left here in town?" Orrville asked.

"You are the only one I've found."

"So—what do we do?"

"We need to leave—*right now*! We'll have to walk. All the car batteries and electric power have been drained. Phone lines and internet have been silenced too. We are completely isolated, cut off from the outside world."

Orrville didn't know what to say. He'd seen movies at the drive-in theater about alien encounters such as this. He never thought or dreamed it could actually happen. Jarred from his thoughts when Pastor McKinnon firmly gripped his shoulder, he noticed the desperation on his face. "Come, my son. We can't stay here."

As they both stood up, their eyes were drawn to the stain glass window near the pulpit. The window exploded in, spraying the altar with shards of colored glass. Crouching down between the pews to shield themselves, both saw the blinding light flooding in through the other windows. Gripping Orrville's chin to draw his eyes toward him, Pastor McKinnon shouted, "Hide in the cellar under the vestibule! Do not open the door until you are sure that you hear no sounds! Go!"

"What about you?" Orrville asked.

"Go!" the pastor once more shouted.

Bewildered at first, Orrville then scurried away up the side aisle to the vestibule. Finding the cellar opening in the floor, no more than a crawl space dug during the Civil War to hide slaves but now used for storage, he climbed down in and was just about to close the doors when more windows suddenly shattered, sending exploding shards of glass across the sanctuary.

Rapidly slamming the door shut, Orrville scooted back into the dark space as far as he could. Pulling his knees up to his chest, he buried his face against them and closed his eyes. Quaking with fear, his chest heaved with every breath, leaving him light-headed and nauseous. Worried for Pastor McKinnon, he wanted to climb out to find him, but fear paralyzed his body. Mumbling, "Please be safe," Orrville began reciting the Lord's Prayer as he waited there in the darkness.

Chapter Three

Thinking he'd hear loud noises from up in the church as he waited, for the longest time Orrville heard nothing after the windows shattered. His hope that Pastor McKinnon would come for him faded there in the darkness with each passing minute. Anxious, wanting to know what happened up there, he crawled close to the door. Inhaling, taking a deep breath for courage, he pressed his hands against the door and slightly pushed up just a sliver to look through. A layer of shattered glass glittered across the main aisle to the altar where the large wooden crucifix had fallen off the wall. Nowhere in sight, though, was the pastor—or anyone else.

Forcing the door completely open, Orrville climbed out and just stood there, glancing around at the damaged sanctuary. "Pastor McKinnon," he lightly called out. Receiving no response, he stepped forward toward the altar. The broken glass crackled under his boots as he made his way down the main aisle. Looking between the rows of pews until he reached the pulpit, he found no traces that the pastor was ever there with him. No footprints or thankfully bloodstains were found. With the exception of the damage to the windows and fallen crucifix, everything seemed just as abandoned as when he first stepped inside.

Backtracking, he left the church. When he was outside, Orrville noticed how the heavy fog still clung to the ground, obscuring the town and surrounding woods from sight. He sat down for a minute to think about where he should go next. Obviously, he needed to get out of town and could only do so on foot. But should he go north or south? And once he arrived at the next town, would he find it the same as Birchwood Hollow now was? If nothing happened there would anyone believe what he'd tell them in claiming space aliens had attacked and taken everyone prisoner? Putting himself in their place, he knew he wouldn't believe such a ridiculous story.

Knowing he wasn't safe staying here at the church, Orrville decided to head south. Bixby, another small town, was roughly a three-mile walk if he stayed on the main road. The trailer he shared with Henry Lee was also on the way. If the pastor was right, Henry Lee wouldn't be there. Remembering the bright lights flooding through the trees, Orrville felt certain of this. He could stop home for a while and maybe put some clothes in a backpack to take with him. He might even try to eat something if his upset stomach would accept food.

Walking down a side street away from the town center, Orrville looked at the darkened windows of the school. Kindergarten through twelfth grade was taught in the same building. In seven months he would have graduated high school with eleven other classmates, ten of which treated him like dirt. He'd been bullied, mostly physical, many times by three of the boys. Henry Lee never asked about the black eyes, cuts, and bruises. Knowing he didn't care, Orrville never told him the how's, when's, or whys of his injuries. They just pretended they didn't happen. As for the girls, they were just as cruel, especially Brennley, a pretty blond-haired girl he'd had a crush on since the sixth grade. Considering she was Mister Verner's daughter, he stayed quiet about how she treated him so he could keep his job at their farm.

Reaching the covered bridge, the fog seemed thicker as he approached the entrance. Hesitant to cross it, he stopped walking and wondered if he should turn back, sticking to the road instead of walking through the woods. But traveling home on the road would take twice as long. And if the aliens were still lurking around, they might find him there. Glancing into the fog bank for traces of headlights and seeing none, Orrville took a deep breath and began walking through the covered bridge.

From the corner of his eye, Orrville noticed midway to the other side, a brightness coming from behind him. Swallowing hard, he bolted ahead to the end of the bridge and then ducked into the high bushes on the roadside. Not once looking back, he kept running through the thick woods until he reached his trailer.

From the outside, his home appeared abandoned and undamaged. He cautiously stepped out from the tree line. Hoping Henry Lee wasn't inside hiding Orrville jogged over to the door and quickly went inside. Expecting to see everything broken and upended, both the kitchen and living room looked spotless as if he or his mom had just cleaned the place. Searching all the rooms, he found no traces of Henry Lee inside.

Orrville believed the aliens would return and knew he couldn't stay here at home. Once in his room, he packed some extra clothes in a backpack and stripped off the still damp clothes and boots he was wearing. Dressing in jeans, a black T-shirt, and sneakers, he grabbed his blue jean jacket and reading glasses before heading to the kitchen. Into his backpack, he stuffed some apples, a package of chocolate chip cookies, and a couple of bottles of water. After cramming his money into his jean's pocket, he went to leave but stopped when a light flashed in the kitchen window.

Peeking out from behind the curtains, his jaw dropped when he saw the surrounding woods flooded with a beaming light, causing the fog to glow. *"Come on,"* he uttered, seeing shadows passing through the light. "Can you give me a break already?" Orrville didn't expect an answer to this question but got one anyway.

Seeing the door thrust open, Henry Lee yelled, *"This way!"* Though shocked at seeing his stepdad, Orrville followed him, running around behind the trailer and back into the woods. *"Keep up! Don't stop!"* Henry Lee urged as the tramped through the dense trees.

Though slowed and hindered by his backpack, Orrville followed his stepdad deeper and deeper into the woods. Stumbling a few times over the rocks hidden in the brush and fallen branches, he managed to keep up with him, even as he staggered down a small ravine. With so many falling colorful leaves in sight, the woods looked like it was dying. The thin veil of patchy fog seeping through the trees looked like a forest fire burned close by.

Trekking to the deepest part of the woods, Henry Lee stopped out of breath, resting his back against the trunk of a large tree. Orrville stopped opposite of him, his lungs aching as he tried catching his breath. "What-is-that?" he forced out.

Pausing to answer, Henry Lee finally said, "Aliens." Taking a few deep breaths, he continued, huffing out, "I watched them…all night…taking people in town."

"So how did you get away from them?"

"Until now they didn't come after me," Henry Lee answered. "I woke up with a splitting headache just after midnight. You weren't anywhere around—which didn't surprise me. Anyway, when I went outside to look for you, I saw the lights and went to see what they were. That's when I saw the people in town walking away like they were zombies or something."

Glancing at his stepdad, Orrville noticed the painful-looking purplish bruise on his forehead. Thinking it was from when he kneed him in the groin and he fell off the bed, Orrville decided not to say anything about it. But not successful in hiding that he'd noticed the bruise, he grew nervous when Henry Lee pointed at it. "Yeah, this was from you," he confirmed. "I don't blame you, though. I deserved it."

"You deserve a whole lot worse," Orrville responded, feeling angry inside.

"You're right," Henry Lee agreed. "I know you won't believe this—"

"I probably won't," Orrville harshly interrupted.

Smirking, glancing away Henry Lee confessed, "You and your mom were the best things that happened to me in my miserable excuse of a life."

"You're right. I don't believe you."

"Not that I've given you any reason to," Henry Lee continued. "Even when I was just a boy, people would point their fingers at me and say, 'that boy isn't right'. I raised more hell than anyone else I knew. I got in trouble with the law *more* times than I care to admit. I reckon I couldn't straighten myself out for nothing." Looking at Orrville, he added, "For what it's worth, I'm sorry, sorry for everything I put you and your mom through."

Though he believed Henry's words were sincere, too much had happened to him and his mom for Orrville to just go ahead and forgive him. He wasn't sure that time would ever come. Wanting to change the subject, Orrville steered their conversation back to the aliens. "You said you woke up in the trailer just after midnight. When I ran away last night, there were blinding lights flooding through the trees. Why do you think they didn't come inside?"

Running his hand over his whiskered face, Henry Lee answered, "I reckon they must have seen you run away. Maybe they thought no one else was inside. Did they chase you?"

"I don't know, *maybe.*"

"Where were you during the night?"

"I hid under the covered bridge leading into town. Then this morning went into town but didn't find anyone until I went to the church. Pastor McKinnon showed up after watching the aliens all night. But before we could leave together—they came and took him—I think. I'd hidden in the storage space in the vestibule. When I climbed out, he was gone. He said we're isolated, no power, phones, or internet."

"He was right," Henry Lee confirmed. "Nothing works."

"Do you think these aliens are just here—or do you think they're in other places?"

Shaking his head, Henry Lee offered, "I don't know."

Thirsty from running, Orrville though about the water bottles he had in his backpack. Though not wanting to share with Henry Lee, understanding that being cruel to his stepdad would solve nothing, he decided on a small kind gesture. "I've got some water in my backpack—if you're thirsty."

Nodding his head, Henry Lee uttered, "Yeah, I am. Thanks."

Peeling the backpack straps off his shoulders, he set it down in the grass in front to fetch the bottles inside. But before he could react, Henry Lee lunged for him, knocking him to the ground. Covered by and flailing under Henry Lee, Orrville yelled when his stepdad pulled his hair and began banging his head against the hard ground. Light-headed after the first thrust, Orrville's sight blurred as Henry Lee continued. His stepdad's weight and his own fatigue played against him. Drained of energy and too disoriented to keep struggling, he couldn't fight anymore. With one final impact of his head against the ground, Orrville's blurred vision darkened until everything faded to black.

Chapter Four

With his head spinning and feeling nauseous, Orrville doubled over and dry heaved a few times, coughing out only spit. Wincing at the pain radiating from the back of his skull, he squeezed his eyes closed and clenched his trembling hands. Reaching out for his backpack, he dug inside one of the outer pockets, looking for his reading glasses and put them on, hoping they would help with his blurred vision. If anything, his glasses made it worse but he decided to keep them on. Looking out, he saw his extra clothes strewn about. Before even checking, he already knew the money in his jeans pocket would be missing, which it was after feeling for it. Releasing a sigh of frustration, he scooted over to the nearest tree to rest his back against its trunk. "How could I have been so stupid?" he mumbled under his breath. "*I hope the aliens find you and eat you for dinner, you bastard*!" Orrville angrily yelled out, hearing traces of his echoing words rebounding.

Aching all over from being pinned down by Henry Lee, it took two unsteady attempts to stand up. Holding on to the tree kept him from swaying too far and falling. Thankful for not seeing any traces of the aliens, he knew in his current condition outrunning them would be impossible. He staggered forward one step and then another trying to hold his balance. *Maybe I have a concussion*, he wondered.

"Orrville Fletcher," he could have sworn he heard his name called in the gentle breeze, the voice sounding like his mom's. But when he listened again, only the call of a whippoorwill resounded in the breeze.

I usually don't hear them 'til sundown, he said to himself. "Now I'm hallucinating," he mumbled aloud, dismissing the idea of hearing his mom's voice. After stuffing his scattered clothes into his backpack, he struggled to pull the straps onto his shoulders. Trudging forward through thick pine trees and bushes, he tried to think of which direction south was. And having no wristwatch with him to tell the time, even the overcast sky offered little help in gaining his bearings. So Orrville just walked straight ahead. *Eventually, I'll find something—I hope*, he silently thought.

Though the day remained cloudy, the air continued with its unseasonable warmth. Wiping the sweat from his forehead, Orrville stopped to remove his jean jacket.

Tying it around his waist, he continued walking.

At least this part of the world hadn't yet been spoiled by the alien invasion. He was thankful for the tranquility in this area of the woods. Although no sunlight shone on the autumn leaves, their colors were only slightly dulled. He heard the sounds of their flapping wings of the birds disturbed from their perch as they took flight. The snaps and crackles of fallen tree branches let him know that animals must be close by.

Before he could finish swinging his neck around and searching the area surrounding him, there rising up on its hind legs from behind a cluster of small pine trees was the largest brown bear Orrville had ever seen. Quaking in terror at the danger he faced, his jaw dropped when he saw the bear's own frightened movements in backing away from him. Struck by how the bear lacked any sort of aggressiveness, Orrville wondered why it was acting so alarmed. *Why would this gigantic bear be scared of me?* The answer to his question, though, came quickly as he thought this through. *Maybe it's not me it's scared of. Maybe it saw something during the night to make it act this way.* Dropping down to its front paws, the bear sniffed deeply before turning to pad away through the thick nearby bushes, leaving Orrville unharmed and standing there alone.

Heading in the opposite direction of the bear, he tracked up to the crest of hill, surprised to see a paved highway just beyond the trees. Careful to climb down through the sliding rocks, he soon reached the side of the paved road. But once there he had no idea which direction it led. Nothing around him looked familiar.

Orrville noticed across the road several deer grazing beyond the field of decaying cornstalks at the edge of the woods. Careful stepping over a deep ditch, he drew closer. His hands worked with the breeze to separate the tall cornstalks blocking his path. Trampling out into the center of the field, the smoke-laced stench rising from the scorched ground clung to the heated air here, forcing him to cover his mouth and nose with his hand. He stood in the center a large circle that clearly looked as if it had been burned during the last few hours. Nothing of the blacken ash covering the ground resembled what once grew here. Only the charred remnants of a scarecrow were even slightly recognizable. Glancing around in all directions, Orrville knew this must have been one of the places where the space aliens had landed during the early hours before dawn. Backing away from this point into the cornstalks, he stumbled over a man's work boot and spotted a woman's discarded pink sweater nearby. He felt certain that some of the people were lured out here to be abducted.

Startled by the ominous caws of several black crows gliding overhead, Orrville gazed up, watching their flight as he continued to move backward away from the burned field. He imagined they were passing a secret between each other and were taking bets to see how long he could last before the aliens would abduct him too.

With his shoes again touching the paved road, his attention was drawn away from the field as he heard the rumble of an engine drawing closer. The sight of the approaching headlights from a long hauler piercing through the fog, had him breathing a sigh of relief. He wanted more than anything to catch a ride from the driver. Waving his arms, he watched the truck slow to a stop. Orrville dared to allow himself a moment of hope.

Leaning out his window, the driver asked, "Where ya headed, Son?"

"Where're you going?" Orrville asked.

"I'm droppin' off this load here of paper products in Knoxville before headin' home just outside Greensburg, Arkansas."

"Knoxville sounds good to me."

"Climb up in," the driver invited him.

"Thanks for giving me a ride, Sir." After closing the door, Orrville timidly asked, "Did you happen to see another guy walking along the road?"

"Shoot, yeah," the driver answered. "But he looked kind of sketchy—so I kept drivin'. Glad I did too. He was none too happy with me I'd say when he started wavin' with only his middle finger. And I thought only city folks did that when I drive too slow?"

Glancing over at the driver, his appearance was unexpected for a long hauler. Short, wrinkled, frail, elderly would best describe him. Orrville had never seen such an old semi driver before. What he noticed the most was the crisp white dress shirt and plaid bowtie he wore.

"Got a hot date tonight?" Orrville asked.

Cackling at his question, the driver responded, "I reckon I do look a might odd for a trucker. My momma, God rest her soul, always told me to take pride in my appearance. She said people will judge ya by what they see—so make them see somethin' good."

"Smart woman," Orrville commented.

"Indeed, she was."

"Would she be angry with you picking up a hitchhiker like me?"

"Naw, she believed in bein' kind to people—and ya seem like a nice, polite boy."

"Thanks."

"If you don't mind me askin', what are ya doin' out here in the middle of nowhere?"

Shrugging his shoulders, Orrville quietly answered, "Just moving on, I guess." Exhaling his nerves away, Orrville cautiously wondered aloud, "Anything—strange going on in the world today?"

"Heck, the whole world is strange to an ol' country boy like me," the driver answered. "You'll have to narrow down your idea of strange."

Not wanting to sound crazy by barking out direct questions about space aliens, instead, Orrville sarcastically responded, "Oh, you know, stuff like the KKK adding black members or Appalachia declaring independence—or an alien invasion."

Laughing, the driver said, "All are unlikely. Shoot, nothin' new out here in the backwoods. By the way, I'm Zebulon

Pike," he offered his name while extending his hand.

"A pleasure to meet you, Mister Pike. I'm Orrville Fletcher."

"Orrville's a mighty fine name for a boy," the driver remarked. "As for me, Mister Pike was my daddy. You can just call me Zeb."

"Zeb, it is."

Noticing Zeb's odd-looking hearing aid, fitting over his ears and having an antenna on the top, Orrville commented, "You're hearing aid looks like something out of a sci-fi movie."

"Shoot, these suckers cost me a pretty penny in Atlanta, but I swear—with them I can hear a fly pass gas on a tin can two miles away. That's why we're steerin' clear of Birchwood Hollow."

Nearly choking on the dryness in his throat, Orrville painfully swallowed and tried calmly asking, "Why? What's going on there?" keeping his eyes on the road ahead.

"I don't right know," Zeb answered. "But when I was drivin' by late last night I picked up some powerful static on my hearin' aids. I tried adjustin' the volume— but the static just got louder as I drove closer. It even left me with my nose bleedin' like someone had just sucker-punched me in the face."

"Did you see anything—odd?"

"I reckon I saw a lot of lightnin'—but it never did storm."

He stayed silent for a while as he thought about what Zeb revealed. Orrville was jarred from his thoughts when Zeb asked, "So—who ya runnin' away from, son? I think ya know ya can trust me."

Without any thought to lie, Orrville answered, "My stepdad."

"That must have been him, the one I passed by on the road, the one ya asked about."

Glancing away out the window, Orrville quietly responded, "Yeah that was him."

"What did he do to ya, son?"

"I don't really want to talk about him if that's all right?"

"I understand." Zeb glanced over at him, and Orrville wasn't surprised when he suggested, "Ya must have been up all night. Ya should get some sleep. Why you're makin' me want to crawl in bed just lookin' at ya."

Resting his head against the window, Orrville closed his eyes and whispered, "Yes, Sir," before falling asleep.

Chapter Five

"Good Morning, Zeb. What can I get you, sugar—other than me and a cheap bottle of wine?" Vivian, his favorite waitress at Smith's Roadside Restaurant flirtingly asked.

"I'll have two pieces of apple pie, a coffee, and a white milk to go," Zeb answered while smiling at her and then winking before glancing at the television in the corner.

"*My*, you sure have an appetite today," she commented after writing down his order.

"Yes, Ma'am. I reckon I'm hungrier than a starving gator at a pool party. Just can't stop thinkin' about that sweet pie ya make."

Choosing not to tell her he'd be sharing this food with the sleeping boy in his truck Zeb didn't want anyone to know about him in case his stepdad was asking around to find out if anyone had seen the boy. But not a minute later, he was confronted by an unexpected twist of truth.

"Excuse me, Sir, might we have a word with you?" Turning around, Zeb tried remaining calm when confronted by two Tennessee state troopers.

"Well, how may I be of service, officers?"

Handing him a wanted bulletin, the taller of the two state troopers responded, "We're conducting a search of this area for a runaway teen involved in a local homicide. Have you seen this boy?"

Glancing down at the picture, Zeb maintained his composure while studying Orrville's face. "No, officers, I can't reckon I've seen this boy. He *looks* like a nice young fella. Who'd he kill?"

"The Sherriff of Birchwood Hollow claims this boy was involved with the murder of his stepdad. That's all we can say at this time."

"As I said, I haven't seen this boy— but I'll be sure to give ya a holler if I see him while headin' toward Knoxville."

"That will be fine, Sir," the second state trooper commented. "Just be prepared to stop. Checkpoints are being set up on all roads leading in and out of the area."

"I will remember that. Thank ya boys for keepin' all us safe," Zeb offered with a smile. Watching the state troopers move on to some men sitting in a booth, Zeb's attention was drawn away from them when the waitress returned with his order.

"Here ya go, sugar," she said to him. "I'll see ya when ya come around next week."

Handing her ten dollars, Zeb remarked, "Keep the change, darlin'," as he carried his pie, coffee, and milk out the restaurant door.

While calmly walking up to his semi, Zeb knew something wrong happened to the boy asleep in his truck. One thing he felt certain of, was that Orrville was no murderer. Considering himself a good judge of character, for just the few minutes he'd spent with the boy, no one could ever convince him that Orrville could be capable of harming anyone. And believing the man he passed on the road was Orrville's stepdad, the likelihood that the boy could have killed his stepdad a mile away and then backtracked that quickly seemed impossible. None of what he heard made any sense, leading him to further wonder what evidence did the Sherriff of Birchwood Hollow have to charge the boy with such a crime, one obviously not committed by him? "There's a *serious* stench of crap in the air," Zeb mumbled to himself.

Approaching his semi, Zeb was startled to see that Orrville wasn't inside. Feeling his pulse racing, he looked around as panic gripped him. The sight of Orrville exiting the door from the outside restroom caused him a moment of anxiety. Fearing the boy might be seen by the state troopers still around, Zeb waved him back. As he jogged over, Zeb whispered, "Get in, quick. The police are lookin' for ya, Son."

Scurrying into the semi cab, Orrville asked, "Why are they looking for *me*?"

"I'll tell ya when we're away from here."

Once he pulled back out onto the road, Zeb told him, "It's far worse, Son. The state police aren't the only ones lookin' for ya. The Sherriff of Birchwood Hollow claims ya killed your stepdad."

"But—that's a lie!" Orrville objected. "He attacked me and stole my money before running off. I swear I didn't kill him!"

"I know ya didn't, Son. And I also know that somethin' aint right in Birchwood Hollow. Son, I need ya to tell me what was goin' on there before ya ran away. I know it might be hard—but ya can trust me."

Shaking and brushing away his tears, Orrville revealed, "Last night after I went to bed, my stepdad came into my room and jumped on me. He was drunk and was looking for the money I got paid with earlier in the day. He gambles away every dollar he can get his hands on."

"Does he gamble with the sherriff?" Zeb interrupted.

"I think so."

"Does your stepdad owe the sheriff money?"

"Yeah, I'm sure he does, him and others. My stepdad never wins anything."

"Now things are makin' sense."

"There's more," Orrville said. "When I ran outside to get away from him, I saw these bright lights outside—flooding through the woods—and shadows. I was scared, so I ran away and hid for the night under a covered bridge leading into town. And—when I walked into town, everyone was gone. I went to the church and our pastor showed up. He claimed everyone had been taken by space aliens during the night."

"Which ya believed?"

"Yeah. I know it sounds crazy. But when we were in the church, the aliens came back and took the pastor. He told me to hide and when I came out, he was gone. I ran home and when I was leaving—the aliens showed up there. My stepdad was also there. We escaped together and ran into the woods. But my stepdad didn't care about the aliens or me. He attacked me again, robbed me, and left me there. *Please*, I'm telling you the truth."

"I reckon an encounter with space aliens is a mighty tall tale to believe—even when told by a pastor. Did ya see them? What were they like?"

"I didn't see them. I only saw shadows and the lights. Please believe me. I'm not lying to you."

"I believe ya, son. Everythin' ya said would explain all the static I heard and the lights I saw last night," Zeb offered. Shaking his head, he continued, "Somethin's just not right, though. Your stepdad aint dead and the state troopers never said *one word* about space aliens in Birchwood Hollow. What the heck are we missin'?"

"I don't know," Orrville mumbled. "What am I going to do?"

Thinking everything through for a moment, Zeb then answered, "The state troopers said that checkpoints were bein' set up leadin' in and out of the area. I'm pretty sure they'll find ya if we try gettin' ya away from here."

"Then just drop me off on the side of the road."

"No," Zeb responded.

"I'll be okay. I'll try walking through the woods to get away."

"And what if they catch ya, either the police of the aliens? Then what?" Zeb argued.

"I don't know."

"Well, I *do*!" Zeb insisted. "A life on the run or hidin' is no life for a boy like ya."

"So what do we do?"

"We're headin' to Birchwood Hollow to find that lyin' sheriff and these space aliens. Somethin's not adding up."

"But nobody's there. I'm sure of it."

"Maybe these *space aliens* are still there—and just maybe they're not all they seem to be."

"But what if they are?"

"Either way we're in a whole heap of trouble. Might as well find out how deep."

"Not you, just me," Orrville said. "Just drop me off on the side of the road and you're out of it. I won't tell anyone you helped me. I promise."

"Not happenin', Son. Sorry, but I'm in this with ya 'til the end. I'm not abandonin' ya."

Soon driving up to a crossroads, Zeb steered his semi toward Birchwood Hollow, believing they wouldn't encounter any checkpoints leading into town. Nearing midday, they approached the town center and he knew it was odd that there was no other traffic on the road. Both of them stayed silent, listening to the droning sounds of the wiper blades moving back and forth wiping the light rain away.

Slowing his semi down the steep hill to the center of town, before Zeb could ask, Orrville directed him, "The police station is near the school."

"Then that's where we're *not* headin'." Driving his semi over to the school parking lot, Zeb carefully parked in between two yellow school buses. The light rain had stopped. Climbing out, he said, "Let's have a look around here. Things just aint addin' up."

"Like what?"

"Do ya remember watchin' movies about space alien invasions?"

"Yeah, a few."

Extending his arms out as they crossed the parking lot, Zeb asked, "So where's the destruction? Look around ya. Why isn't anythin' burned to the ground or reduced to rubble? Why does this place appear like a deserted ghost town?"

"I don't know—but all the church windows were shattered when I was there with Pastor McKinnon."

"Take me to the church," Zeb urged.

They walked up to the church and both stopped dead in their tracks. Orrville's claim that the windows were shattered had been proven false when staring at the dark undamaged windows. Shaking his head, Orrville mumbled, "But-but-I-don't-understand. The windows were—all broken."

"Come on," Zeb said. "Let's go inside."

Pulling open the unlocked doors, both quietly entered the vestibule and then stepped further into the sanctuary. Pointing toward the altar, Orrville's jaw dropped with him uttering, "The wooden crucifix had fallen off the wall—but now it's back in place. This can't be." Staggering back he sat down on one of the pews. He kept his eyes on the pulpit as he broke down. "I don't—understand," he choked out. "I'm not lying."

"I believe ya, Son," Zeb said as he sat down next to Orrville. Placing his hand on Orrville's shoulder to comfort him, Zeb was about to offer his thoughts but stopped when he spotted something glistening on the floor under the pew in front of them. Bending down, he reached under it, carefully picking up a sliver of blue stain glass, jagged on all edges.

Zeb stood up and walked over to the stain glass window next to the pulpit. Glancing over the intricate design, he focused his attention solely on the pattern's blue colored glass. He noticed a slim shaft of light piercing the lower left blue glass. Not only did the color match, but when the sliver of stain glass was placed over the hole, it fit perfectly, like the last piece of a jigsaw puzzle.

Never a believer in things being just a coincidence, Zeb wandered around the sanctuary, studying each of the tall stain glass windows. What struck him most was how polished and clean each one appeared as if freshly washed...or new.

Walking slow back over to Orrville, Zeb whispered, "We should go now."

Sniffling and brushing his tears away, Orrville asked, "Where—to next?"

With his tone calm, Zeb answered returning to the vestibule, "Anywhere but here. Come on with ya."

They stepped outside, and bright lights blinded both. More startled and afraid than he ever thought he could be, Zeb stood paralyzed trying to shield his eyes. Shadowed movements then appeared along with a creeping mist coming closer and closer.

Chapter Six

When Orrville opened his eyes, everything appeared blurred and his throat hurt as he tried to swallow. Feeling groggy and light-headed, the bitter taste in his mouth made him feel nauseous. A chill ran along his spine as if someone had walked over his future grave, something his mom once claimed caused a person chills. His hands started to twitch and his body began trembling. *"Where am I?"* he murmured under his breath.

His ears picked up a light droning buzz—he was sure it sounded like a machine of some kind. As he regained his senses, he wondered what kind of machine was making the buzzing sound. He remembered walking outside the church with Zeb, and there were blinding lights that burned his eyes. He tried shielding his eyes from it. And then there was the strange smell coming from the smoke. It reminded him of breathing in the air at a doctor's office—it didn't smell like fire smoke. Then he felt sleepy and drained of energy. That was the last thing he recalled before waking up now.

"Zeb," he whispered and waited, but heard no response. Wiping the sleepiness from his eyes with his hands, Orrville blinked several times forcing his sight to improve. But there wasn't anything to see other than a faint blinking light overhead and the darkness surrounding the table, or whatever, he lay upon. The surface felt cold against his bare back. He just now realized his T-shirt was gone. Touching his chest, he felt the wires running from patches covering both nipples. Yanking at them, he winced in pain when they pulled free from his skin. As he sat up, his head spun from a sudden headache coming on.

Swinging his feet around, he touched his toes to the cold surface of the floor. Shivering he realized his shoes were missing too. But before he could stand a hand covered his mouth as an arm came around his chest from behind, holding him firm as the air rushed from his lungs. While his heart nearly exploded through his heaving chest, he listened as a male voice quietly rasped, "*Shut up.*"

Orrville could see nothing but blackness around him. Already quaking with fear, his terror intensified as his body was forcibly dragged back, away from what he sat on. Then something even more unexpected happened. The one with him suddenly hugged him, holding him close. Though still frightened, he heard the man whisper, "Follow me."

He held on to the man's hand as he was being led away down the dark hallway. A dim light at the end lit their way as they walked toward it. He felt moisture on the cold concrete floor as he breathed in the musty dampness in the air. As they drew closer to the end, Orrville noticed the man's silhouette and panic set in when he recognized whom he was with. Releasing his hold on his stepdad's hand, Orrville staggered back from him.

"I'm not the one you should be scared off," Henry Lee mumbled.

Reeling with fear, he looked at Henry Lee covered in dark filth. Orrville wasn't sure he'd ever seen his stepdad appear worse. Henry Lee's eyes were wide open, shifting as if gripped by paranoia. And his hands shook as they did when he came off one of his alcohol binges, but he didn't smell of beer, just the stench of strong body odor. "We'll be safe here in these tunnels—at least for a while," Henry Lee said. "I've been learning my way around. I know how to keep away from them."

"What is this place?" Orrville asked.

"It's an old abandoned World War II ammunition depot, just a few miles away from town."

"How did we get here?"

"The aliens brought us here. They're all over the place."

"What do they look like?"

"The same as they did before, just shadows in the light."

"How'd you get away from them?"

"I played possum. I let the aliens think I'd passed out like the rest of them."

"Like the rest of who?"

"The people from town. I think they're all here."

"Where?"

"Scattered all over. It's strange how they did it. They've like separated everyone into different groups, boys and girls, men and woman, even by age—young and old."

"Are they okay?"

"If you call passed out and lying flat on their backs okay, then yeah."

"Why?"

"It's just like in the movies. They've snatched everyone and are now preparing to do their weird experiments."

"But what about me? Why was I alone and not with the other boys?"

"They just brought you in. Maybe they didn't have time yet to take you to the others."

"You saw them bring me in here?"

"Yeah."

"Did they bring an old guy in with me?"

"No, not that I saw. Just you."

Startled by traces of light shining from the dark end of the other tunnel, Henry Lee whispered, "Hurry, they're coming!" When his stepdad reached for his arm, Orrville kept away from him by stepping back into the shadows. "What are you doing, you idiot! They'll find you!" his stepdad hissed. But Orrville ignored this warning, instead, turning and running away from him, back into the darkness.

Trusting his stepdad was a mistake Orrville intended not to make again. Too many times before Henry Lee showed his true colors, pretending to protect him—the most recent being in the woods. Recalling another time after Henry Lee married his mom, when they went camping together there was an encounter with a hungry bear, proving this theory just as the woods did. Henry Lee had taken off running, leaving Orrville behind. His stepdad was best at selfishness and wouldn't think twice to sacrifice him to the aliens so he could survive.

Chilled water from the tunnel's floor splashed over his bare feet as he ran further into the darkness. After painfully colliding with a wall when he reached an unexpected intersection, Orrville fell to his knees, wincing from the throbbing aches radiating from his shoulder and head. Glancing in both directions, he wasn't sure which way to go. He listened and heard nothing, confirming his belief that Henry Lee wouldn't sacrifice himself to help. Otherwise, he would have followed behind to ensure his stepson's safety. *I'm on my own*, Orrville thought to himself, a truth he already knew.

Orrville moved at a slower pace, tracing his hand over the coarse texture of the tunnel wall to guide him. Even though he found nothing ahead or behind him, his fear ran rampant offering little comfort. But he also heard no noises ahead or behind him, allowing him to remain calm at least for the moment.

Thinking things through, the fact that Henry Lee continued to escape from the space aliens provided Orrville with a sense of relief. No one would ever consider his stepdad to be a smart man, so if the aliens couldn't capture a dumb ass such as him, then a smart boy such as himself might have a better chance to not only keep away from them but find a passage out. But then what? Run and get the police? Who would believe someone accused of committing a murder trying to warn every one of an alien invasion? No, getting the police would be the last thing he would do. With so many in town looking down at him for being poor, maybe they deserved what they got. Orrville wondered if he could just slip away and find a new life far from here where no one knew him. Maybe an alien invasion was exactly what he needed.

Startled to find a set of doors on his right, he pushed one in and a flickering overhead light turned on. Orrville's jaw dropped when the room revealed those inside. He found several boys his age lying unconscious on tables lined in the center of the room. Each had been stripped bare of their shoes and shirts and had wires attached to their nipples similar to the ones he found on himself when he woke up. But there was something else. Next to the first table a much smaller table sat. Wandering over to it, Orrville couldn't believe his eyes at finding a handwritten note and a black marker. He read the following instruction to himself. *'Do it. You know you want to. They deserve it.'* Orrville understood what was written yet had no idea which one of the boys confessed to what they did or who had watched them do it. Thinking back, he recalled what had happened after gym class the week before.

Having survived a brutal game of dodgeball, Orrville was confronted by four boys in his class as he headed into the locker room to change. Surrounding him, each took turns commenting on how poor he was and how his stepdad's gambling was the talk of the town. Three of the boys' dads were owed money by Henry Lee, with none having been paid a dime. So with their dads' blessings, according to them, Orrville was to carry a message home to his stepdad, but not just any message.

Forcing him to the floor and stripping him down to his underwear, the boys then took a black marker and wrote threats and profanity over every exposed part of Orrville. They then pushed him out the locker room door into the busy hallway for the teachers and other students to see. Turning a blind eye to him, none of the teachers stepped in to help. As for the other kids, their laughter fueled Orrville's embarrassment and humiliation. He remembered running out the main school doors just as the lunchtime bells rang. And if all this wasn't enough, when he got home

Henry Lee exploded in anger, dragging him into an ice-cold shower to scrub off the messages.

Picking up the black marker, Orrville's hand trembled as he thought more of the disgusting words the boys had written on his skin. Having so many times been a victim of their abuse, he always wondered what it would be like to get revenge. Would it make him feel any better? Would it change things? Or would he be inviting more trouble for himself? With them now unconscious Orrville knew he had his chance. But not knowing the aliens plans for these boys and the others, he wasn't sure they'd ever see what he would write. So, instead of seeking retribution for what they did to him, he backed away and left through the door he entered through. Maybe the best revenge he could seek was just getting away. With luck, he'd never see any of them again.

Returning to the dark hallway, Orrville headed to the right and came to a halt when he saw traces of light in the next tunnel. Turning in the other direction, his heart stopped, with his next breath rushing from his lungs as he heard footsteps drawing closer to him. Expecting to see Henry Lee cowering there in the darkness, Orrville quaked in fear when a man using night vision goggles appeared before him.

Dressed all in black, he looked more like a shadow than a living person. Watching the man place a finger to his lips, Orrville was surprised when he waved at him to follow. Glancing back at the approaching lights, Orrville decided to go with the man. He trailed behind him down another dark hallway until they reached a solid steel door.

Watching the man punch a numeric code onto a keypad, they waited until the door opened and then entered into a dark room. Orrville's jaw dropped at the surveillance video monitors as the door closed behind them. Moving toward the closest one, he was stunned to see the inside of the church. Glancing toward the other monitors, each showed different parts of the town, both the inside of homes and buildings and the outside. Even more disturbing, though, was when Orrville noticed a monitor that showed the interior of his trailer on the outskirts of town. "Everyone was being watched," he mumbled under his breath. "That was…how they knew to find me."

Turning around to face the man still standing by the door, Orrville asked, "Are you working with the space aliens?"

"No," the man quietly responded.

"Who are you?"

"I'm John Howard. I'm…your dad."

Chapter Seven

Stunned when he heard the man reveal his identity, Orrville shook his head in disbelief.

"It's true," the man said. John took off his night vision goggles and pulled down the hood of his black jacket, revealing his smiling face. Orrville noticed that they didn't share similar features. This further fueled his distrust. "Did your mom ever talk about me?" John wondered.

"No. Whenever I asked her about my real dad she'd just say that he ran out on her and that she didn't like thinking about him. She never said anything else."

"I guess I can understand why," John offered. "I kept so much hidden from her. I had to. It was the only way to keep you both safe."

Hearing these words, Orrville gave him a crooked smirk, shaking his head. "If you really are my dad—then just which part of our lives were you keeping us safe from?" Pointing at the surveillance monitor showing the main inside school hallway, Orrville continued, "Were you keeping me safe from the bullies when I went to school? Were you keeping us safe when we lost our house and had to move into that run-down trailer on the edge of town—or when we had barely enough to eat and they were threatening to turn off the power?" Teary-eyed, Orrville asked, "Were you—keeping me safe from Henry Lee? Were you? I find your idea of "*keeping us safe*"—pretty hard to believe."

Seeing John take a step toward him, Orrville backed away. "I'm so sorry, Son."

"I'm not—your son!" Orrville corrected him. "I don't know who you are—but I do know that you're not my dad. A dad doesn't abandon his kid. A dad keeps his son safe. You never did... so don't make claims about being something you're not."

"I did try to keep you and your mom safe," John argued, sounding frustrated. "Just not in ways you could see."

"Really? How?"

Motioning with his hands, John responded, "I kept you safe from all this."

"What is all this?"

"A lie, unlike any other."

"What do you mean?"

"I mean...that everything you've seen is a lie. There's no space alien invasion. It's all an elaborate hoax. We're standing in one of the surveillance rooms of a secret government testing site. And we're in the middle of one of the biggest mind-altering experiments the government has ever initiated."

"Why would they be testing anything mind-altering?"

"To use against America's enemies."

"So the people of Birchwood Hollow, are America's enemies?"

"No, just necessary volunteers for testing this new weapon."

"Chemical weapons aren't new," Orrville reminded him.

"This type doesn't fall under any outlawed chemical weapon category."

"So that makes all this okay."

"No, but it can't be stopped."

Orrville's distrustful glance didn't ease the tension between them. John understood this and said, "I want to show you something." Wandering over to a computer console, John typed on the keyboard, changing the surveillance camera view on one of the monitors to show a different location, one Orrville quickly recognized. Moving closer, Orrville looked at the secluded knoll where he'd spread his mom's ashes, her favorite place in the woods. He felt his heart sink in his chest as he looked at this quiet place surrounded by fall's most breathtaking autumn-colored leaves.

"I know you're scared and hurt by everything. I understand how you feel. I really do."

"I doubt you could," Orrville mumbled under his breath.

"I was abandoned by my drug-addicted parents in Cleveland, Ohio when I was four years old," John revealed. "No one wanted to adopt me... so I grew up in a boy's home where I was beaten almost every day. When I turned eighteen, I enlisted in the army. While in basic training, I was approached to take part in a secret branch of the military. I was chosen because I had no family. Anyway, I wasn't actually given much of a choice, so I said yes to a lifetime commitment underground. I ended up here at this hidden military site. My job was to watch the monitors, keep track of things in and around Birchwood Hollow and report my findings.

"One day when I was watching, I spotted this beautiful young woman having a picnic by herself at this knoll in the woods. I fell in love with your mom that first moment I saw her. I couldn't stop looking at her. Every day she'd come there for a picnic that spring, even on rainy days. I knew I had to meet her—but I wasn't allowed to leave. So, one day I took a risk and breached security and went for a walk in the woods and met your mom there. Macey was so pretty, so easy to talk to. She had these incredible dreams for her future. She told me she wanted to be a writer and travel the world."

Orrville remembered her saying this to him, telling him these were her heart's secret desires she shared with only him and his dad.

"I kept meeting her there and after a few weeks our friendship turned romantic," John confessed. "A month later your mom told me she was pregnant. At first, she was scared, but I couldn't have been happier. We made plans to run away together. She wanted to go to Paris."

"So what happened?" Orrville asked after John grew silent.

"I was careless one day and my commander discovered that I was sneaking out of the facility. I was sent to solitary confinement for a month. I was told if I ever tried to sneak out again that I would be shot in the head along with anyone they found me with. When I was released, I was forced to return to my duties. I wanted to run away and find your mom. My way out from before, though, was blocked by a large concrete barricade with no other way in or out other than through the heavily guarded main entrance. I was never able to leave here to find her. I know she thought I abandoned her…but I had no choice. Even if I would have found another way out, by doing so I would have risked both her life and yours. I couldn't live with myself if anything happened to either of you."

"But something did happen to us," Orrville burst out. "We hardly managed to survive until Henry Lee came along, and then things got worse." Unable to hold back his tears, Orrville's chest heaved as he added, "My-mom-died-and—Henry Lee made my life a living hell. That's what happened."

Shaking his head, John uttered, "I know. I'm so sorry. All I could do…was watch. Believe me. Your mom was the only woman I ever loved. It killed me seeing her die and watching how cruel everyone was to you."

Though brimming with anger, a part of him felt sad for John. But Orrville still saw John as a stranger, wanting to trust him—but not yet sure he could. Deciding to change the conversation, Orrville asked, "So, what's so special about Birchwood Hollow? Why has the government been watching us all these years?"

"Birchwood Hollow is about as remote a place you could find in Appalachia," John confirmed. "The only people who come to town are either lost or live here. This was the perfect place for the government to choose for secret testing on a mass scale."

"I still don't understand what they're testing."

"Mind-altering drugs and their effects on human bodies of all ages. Since the 1950s, the government has secretly been experimenting with different drugs on humans. These aren't the kind of drugs that cure anything. They're the kind that can erase a person's memories or alter their behavior. I don't think many people would freely agree to be a part of these kinds of tests."

"But you said some have been tested with them."

"Not willingly. Oh sure, they've conducted their experiments with homeless people, but they don't tend to be as smart as others in most cases. Some even suffer behavioral and mental conditions that corrupt the results. No, they wanted more educated people who wouldn't think for a moment about agreeing to be studied and examined. So the government started what they call the Harvest Protocol."

"What does this have to do with Harvest?"

"It's not the kind of harvest you're thinking of," John corrected him. "Not harvesting crops, but people, people traveling alone on lonely roads at night in the middle of nowhere. You've seen science fiction movies about stuff like this. With every abduction, the government makes it look like space aliens are taking the people. This way, if the drugs fail when testing, all these people will be left with are unbelievable tales about being kidnapped by creatures from outer space. We call this Harvest Fever. When was the last time anyone believed such nonsense?"

"How long are the people gone when they're taken?"

Shrugging his shoulders, John answered, "A person might be gone as short as a few hours or as long as a year or more. Some don't even come back. Ever heard of the Bermuda Triangle? Think it's funny how many ships and airplanes have gone missing over the years? That was the first government testing site. They shut it down after too many people asked too many questions and started snooping around."

"Unbelievable," Orrville mumbled. "Next you're gonna tell me Big Foot is real." John chuckled when he heard his comment. Thinking for a moment, Orrville asked, "Was it you who kept me from being taken with the other boys my age after I was brought here?"

"No. When you were brought in, your stepdad caused a commotion, forcing the soldiers to go after him."

"That doesn't really make sense. Henry Lee has never cared about me. Why would he bother?"

"I'm not sure. But what I do know is that they won't stop until they've captured you both. The Government doesn't like loose ends that risk exposing this place."

"How do they know they got everyone else in town?"

"By the census taken last year and the town's records of birth and death since then."

"How did they get everyone to come willingly with them?"

"For months now the government has been tainting the town's drinking water with an experimental hallucinogenic drug that triggers a hypnosis reaction when a certain siren at the fire station sounds out. The soldiers then went into town to collect anyone who couldn't walk, babies, old people."

Orrville remembered Henry Lee commenting on a strange sounding siren when they were eating dinner. He also remembered Pastor McKinnon mentioning this too. "So that's why those of us out on the edge of town weren't affected. We don't have city water."

"Right. For people like you, the soldiers used fog machines emitting a hallucinogenic mist. You, your stepdad, and the pastor, by the way, were the only ones who escaped from the soldiers until you were all captured later."

"What about Zeb, the old semi driver I was with?"

"He doesn't live in Birchwood Hollow so he wasn't part of the experiments. Don't worry about him. He's fine. They gave him a diluted form of a mind-altering drug and took him to a truck stop just outside Knoxville to sleep it off. When he wakes up, he'll have a terrible headache and won't remember what happened over the last day or so."

Sighing with relief, Orrville said, "I'm glad he'll be okay. He was nice to me. Not many people were."

"I know," John mumbled, looking guilty and embarrassed. But there was something off in his expression, something forced and maybe even fake.

"So what now?"

"Well, fortunately for us, your stepdad is causing a lot of problems for the soldiers here. This makes things easier for us. I know of a place we can hide out for a while, a place where you can eat and sleep. I'll get you some shoes and other clothes to wear."

"Then you'll help me escape from here," Orrville added.

"What do you mean?" John asked.

Again troubled by how the expression on John's face changed, his eyes grew disturbingly large, Orrville's pulse raced in fear when he heard his next words. "Son, it's way too dangerous out there. You're gonna stay here with me. I'm gonna take care of you, *right here*. You'll never be alone again. I promise."

Chapter Eight

Watching John's fingers shaking at his side, Orrville guessed he might be nervous. When he saw John's right hand disappear in his pocket, Orrville knew something wasn't right and felt threatened. "Come on, Son. We need to get out of here before the soldiers find us. Follow me."

He hesitated to move. John shifted his weight appearing tense, clearly anxious to get moving. "I want to get out of this place," Orrville mumbled.

Shaking his head, John let out a chuckle then harshly reprimanded him. "Now, you need to listen to me. You need to be a good boy and do as I say. Do you understand?"

Believing John was only moments away from becoming unhinged, Orrville thought of his words and carefully responded, "I'm—sorry, Dad. I'm just scared." Though in truth fearful of going with John, he knew he'd need to lie until the right moment when he could run away. "I didn't mean to make you mad."

With a deep exhale, John seemed to release the tension gripping him. Smiling, he offered, "It's okay, Son. I'm scared too. But we'll be fine as long as you listen to me."

"Yes, Sir."

"That's a good boy. Now come on. We don't have much time."

Orrville stayed close to John as they crept through one dark tunnel and then another. When they reached an open, lit area with metal stairs and ladders, Orrville guessed this might be his best chance to break away. When John had climbed halfway up a ladder, Orrville bolted down the dark tunnel to his left.

"Hey! Come back!" John bellowed, the echoes of his voice deafening to hear. Not once did Orrville turn around, knowing he'd be in danger if he did.

Brushing his fingers along the cold concrete walls, Orrville felt his way deeper into the maze of tunnels. He stopped once to listen for signs of John following him. But the noise he heard sounded more like rats scampering away than someone rushing toward him. Though relieved he'd lost John, Orrville was concerned that he'd also got himself lost. Following tunnel after tunnel, he knew he couldn't backtrack to a point he remembered from before. Maybe if he were lucky, he'd find a sign of anything that would lead him to a place he'd already been. Nothing he'd seen so far and no one he'd encountered offered him any hope of escape.

Sloshing through a thin layer of water, his bare feet grew colder, sending a chill through his body. As he pressed on he noticed the fluid reflection of dim light on the water's surface near the end of the tunnel. Orrville's breath rushed from his body as he glanced further ahead, spotting a body slumped down against the wall. Cautiously approaching, his first thought was the person might be dead. With the slightest shift of the person's head, Orrville stopped walking when the person reached out a hand to him. "Help—me," a man's voice faintly whispered.

Slowly stepping toward the man, Orrville watched as he turned his head away from him. The glow of the dim light revealed the man's badly bruised and bloodied face. Kneeling next to him, Orrville asked, "Who did this to you?"

"My-commander," the man choked out.

"What's his name?"

"Captain…John Howard."

Now trembling, Orrville asked, "Why did he hurt you?"

"He's…insane. Too…many years down here."

Orrville was uncertain whether he should trust this man but knew his belief was confirmed that something wasn't right about John Howard. But he couldn't just leave him here. Maybe this man could help him escape, considering what happened to him.

"I'm not sure what I can do for you."

"Help…me…stand, please," the man breathlessly pleaded.

Orrville allowed the man to drape his arm around his shoulder. Careful in helping him up, Orrville continued holding on to him. "We…need to go…right," the man mumbled.

Though slow and unsteady, with Orrville's help the man led them down three more tunnels until they came to a set of metal doors. "What is this?" Orrville asked.

"Barracks," the man responded.

"Won't there be others inside?" Orrville nervously uttered.

"No," the man answered. "They're out…pretending to be—"

"Space aliens," Orrville finished his sentence.

"Yeah."

Pushing the doors open, the man pointed toward a hallway leading right. "Help-me-down-to-the-utility-closet-at-the-end."

Passing by open doors, glancing into small rooms he found them full of bunk beds and not much else, Orrville wondered how anyone could live for so long in such conditions. Nowhere in sight was there anything of comfort. No televisions or computers sat on desks or tables. The soldiers appeared to enjoy no access to the outside world. Even the warm air he breathed in left traces that it wasn't fresh but instead tainted with an unrecognizable sterile odor.

Orrville helped the man walk toward the solid metal door at the end. Pressing his hand against the hot surface, Orrville pushed the door in and the two of them disappeared inside. Once the door had closed behind them the man urged, "Help-me-to-the-space-behind-these-two-large-boilers."

By the time they passed through the heated mist being released from the boiler tanks, Orrville felt his body dripping with sweat when they reached the spot the man asked to be helped to. Orrville's shock at seeing a lantern lighting a cot and sleeping bag must have been apparent. "It's the…only place…I could find…to hide," the man revealed as Orrville helped him sit down on the cot. "No one comes in here."

Kneeling next to the cot, he watched the man wincing in pain as he held a hand to his rib cage. The man appeared more injured in the light than Orrville first thought. A bloody cut on his forehead seemed deep. Both eyes were black and severely swollen shut. Blood had seeped down from the cuts on his lips. Coughing hard, the man wheezed to catch his breath as he wiped bloody spit dripping from the corner of his mouth.

"Your commander did this to you?"

"Yeah," the man answered.

"Why?"

Watching the man swallow hard and seeing tears stream from his eyes, Orrville noticed how the man struggled in answering, "I…had…to stop him."

"From taking everyone in town and doing all these tests?"

"No.   I-had-to-stop-him-from-hurting-you."

With his hand quaking, the man reached under his sleeping bag and pulled out a small black-covered book similar to the book of poems his mom had. Without saying anything the man handed the book to Orrville.

Hesitant at first to take it from him, Orrville silently did so after seeing the desperation in the man's expression. Holding the book in his hand, Orrville studied the cover so familiar to him. He also noticed a sliver of something showing from inside the cover. Opening the book, Orrville's jaw dropped as an old picture of his mom and the man fell into his palm. It must have been taken at a carnival, judging from the background. They both looked like they were on a Ferris wheel, holding hands and smiling.

Cautiously, he looked at the man. Orrville recognized the similarities they shared—hair, eye color, and the shape of their jaws. "Are-you-my-dad?" Orrville asked.

"Yeah, I am."

"But why did—"

"He's out of his mind. He's…been down here too long. We…all have," Orrville's real dad quietly uttered.

"How does he know all about me?"

"He threatened to hurt you—if I didn't—tell him everything."

"What about all that stuff he said about meeting my mom and his past? Was any of it real?"

"I didn't…hear what he said…to you. But…if it's what…I think, then yeah. You…just heard it all…from the wrong man."

"What's your name?"

"Mark Fletcher."

"Mark is my middle name," Orrville revealed, causing his dad to smile. But this faded when he locked eyes with Orrville.

Though he still struggled with breathing, Mark's words sounded less forced. "I'm—sorry about everything. I—wish I could make things better. I loved your mom. I know she thought I abandoned her, but I got caught, and had to pay the price to keep you both safe. I thought I was being careful but I failed."

"Was John Howard the one who stopped you from being with my mom?"

"Yeah. At first, I thought he was just doing his job, but later I found out how jealous he was. He found out about me and your mom and wanted to take my place. But—I stopped him."

"How?"

"I destroyed my secret way out of here."

"Now the only way in or out is through the heavily guarded entrance."

"No," Mark corrected him. "There are three other ways, but only two might work for you. There's no time left to think these through. You have to decide now."

"What other ways can we get out of here?"

Shaking his head, Orrville knew his dad's response before he uttered it. "Not *we*—but *you*."

"I can't leave you here."

"We don't have a choice," Mark responded. Pulling his hand away from his rib cage, Mark revealed a bloody stab wound Orrville hadn't noticed before.

Orrville's heart sank within his chest as his words were strangled deep in his throat. Feeling overwhelmed by everything, he blankly stared at his dad, not knowing how to help.

"It's okay. It doesn't hurt anymore," Mark whispered, trying to smile. Reaching over, he touched Orrville's cheek. "I'm sorry. You have to go."

On the edge of falling apart, Orrville choked out, "How?"

Swallowing deep, appearing to suffer a spike in pain, his dad answered, "You-can't-let-John Howard find you. He won't let you leave. And-you-can't-let-your stepdad find you. He'll just use you to get away. Son, there's three ways you can get out. On the other side of these boilers is a thin air shaft leading up to the surface. I'm sure you could fit it, but it's about a half mile up with nothing to hold on to once you're inside. And if you slip, there's nothing to stop your fall."

"What are other the ways?"

"You could let the other soldiers find you. Maybe you'll be included with the testing like the others. But John Howard could take you just as well. I think it's too much of a risk to do that."

"What's the third way?"

"I have a syringe, holding a drug inside that causes paralysis and reduced heartbeat and breathing. Once injected, it would make you seem like you're dead. The effects would last about twelve hours. If you choose this, inject the drug into your arm and find a place where the soldiers will discover your body. When someone here dies, they take the body outside and dump it in the woods. You'd wake up there and then escape."

"Wouldn't John Howard try to stop them?"

"No. He doesn't know about this drug. Like the others, he'll believe you're dead."

Staying quiet for a minute, Orrville thought of each option, none of which he felt comfortable with. There had to be another way, one that would lead them both to escape.

"None of these will work," Orrville argued. "I can't leave you here."

"You have to. I don't want anyone to hurt you again."

"Dad, please—"

"No," Mark interrupted. "I spent a lifetime failing you and your mom. I-won't-do-it again. It sure is nice, though, to hear you call me dad."

"Please, don't ask me to leave you."

"You have to. Go on. I'm begging you," Mark insisted, nearly in tears.

"I can't."

"Yes, you can. You're so much stronger that I ever was. You can do this."

He tried to hand the book of poems back to him, Mark smiled, but refused to take it. "Then—at least keep the picture," Orrville offered.

Clearly reluctant, nonetheless Mark took the picture and in exchange handed Orrville the syringe. "Take care," he whispered. "Get as far away as you can. Don't look back."

Nodding his head, Orrville couldn't speak as he stood up. Tears stung his eyes as he looked at his dad one last time before turning away. When he reached the end of the closest boiler, he thought about turning back, but he knew he wouldn't leave if he did.

Chapter Nine

Finding the air shaft his dad spoke of, Orrville reached up, feeling the hot smooth surface inside. He wanted an easier climb to get in, so he searched around for something sturdy he could position under the opening to step on. Dragging an old dusty desk away from a wall, he set it under the opening and stood up on it. Reaching for the handle, he tightened his grip and pulled himself up his feet dangling against the inside of the air shaft. Sweating and panting in the thin heated air, Orrville struggled not to slip. Pressing his bare back against the smooth surface, he used his hands and began his slow ascent up the dark shaft. The heated metal scorched his back and feet but he ignored the sting, no worse than a sunburn.

Seeing no light shining down from above, Orrville wondered if it was dark outside or if there was a covering at the top of the air shaft. Either way, the pitch-blackness made him feel disoriented and unable to tell how far he'd climbed up. Wanting to avoid panic as he continued on he tried thinking of what would come after his escape. It was easy to convince himself not to stay in Birchwood Hollow. His memories of the town, although already bad, would forever be linked to this government conspiracy. And knowing everyone in town had been forced to take part, Orrville had no idea how he could look at them again without wondering if any of the people would remember what happened. If they did, the others might think they were crazy should they openly talk about what they experienced. And he also worried that the government might know of his escape and could target him for what he knew. The risk was too great to stay. Leaving is the only way to survive, he thought.

Next, he wondered where he should go. Orrville knew of an uncle in Florida he'd never met. From what his mom said, she and her mom had a falling out before he was born. Though she never said what it was about, he wondered if this was due to her getting pregnant by someone who abandoned her. She seldom ever spoke of her brother and parents. Orrville guessed she was determined to make it on her own without their help. And maybe they never offered to help her. Possibly in the heat of the moment, things were said that couldn't be taken back. Having no relationship with his uncle or grandparents, if they were still alive, Orrville had no intention of finding them. They were strangers to each other and would remain that way.

Orrville's progress slowed as his exhaustion weighed on him. He rejected the thought of resting for a minute, worried if he relaxed his body then he would slip and fall. Every muscle ached and the sweat pouring down him did nothing to cool his skin. Wanting a drink in the worst way, he licked his dry lips, but not even his tongue had any moisture.

A stray gust of cold air cooled him from above, offering him the first glimmer of hope there in the confined shaft. But his slow progress and fatigue conflicted with this. Orrville's strained muscles began shaking, though he tried to remain calm. "I-can-do-this," he mumbled, almost breathless. Panting hard, Orrville attempted to quicken his pace. The stress on his body, however, betrayed his resolve to reach the top. Shuddering uncontrollably, Orrville's foot lost its hold, sending him sliding down the air shaft.

The desktop below broke his fall as his body fell hard against it, cracking on the hard wood top. Unable to stop, Orrville rolled off onto the concrete floor, knocking the wind out of him when his back slammed against the surface. Struggling to catch his breath, Orrville noticed glittering stars before his eyes and a sharp pain radiating from his skull. Disoriented, it took him a few minutes for the fog in his mind to clear enough for him to recall what had just happened and where he was.

Sitting up, the room spun in his view, forcing Orrville to close his eyes for a minute. When he opened them again, he still felt light-headed, but his surroundings looked mostly clear. Moving a little, his body shook as every muscle ached. Surprisingly, though, nothing seemed broken until he tried standing up. The throbbing from his left ankle robbed him of his breath. Scared to look down, once he did Orrville felt relieved that it didn't seem broken, but maybe strained and definitely bruised.

Hobbling over to lean against the desk, he looked around, watching the steam from the boilers and the flickering of the dim overhead light. Glancing back up at the air shaft, Orrville knew he couldn't try escaping this way again, leaving him with only two other options. He rejected the thought of just giving himself up. If his dad was right, by injecting himself with the syringe in his pocket, the government agents, thinking he'd died, would dispose of his body in the woods. From there, he could escape after the drug wore off.

Remembering his dad was close, Orrville hobbled over to his hiding place past the boilers. Rounding the corner, Orrville halted his steps, noticing his dad's blank stare. He had hoped to talk to him again, but realized his dad was dead. His heart was heavy with regret at seeing this. He felt sadness for his dad and how lonely his life and death had been. But Orrville knew that now was not the time to wonder about what life would have been like for him and his mom if his dad had escaped from here and taken them with him far away. His mom always told him to never worry about how things could have been, only focus on now and the future.

Moving closer, Orrville reached over to close his dad's eyes. Seeing the picture still gripped in his dad's hand, he pried it free from his fingers and pulled the book of poems from his back pocket. Returning the picture to a place inside the book, Orrville forced it back into his pocket before draping a blanket over his dad. "I'm sorry," he whispered. "But—maybe—you'll see my mom now. Tell her—I miss her," he added, unable to stop his tears from falling.

Limping away, Orrville retraced the steps he thought his dad followed leading them to this boiler room. The air in the dark tunnels felt much cooler against his exposed skin as he limped and padded along, using his fingers to trace against the walls to help lead him. For the longest time, each turn he navigated yielded continued darkness. There was no one around. Orrville believed he'd become even more lost than before. He worried he might never find his way out or meet up with the government agents acting like aliens. He also feared injecting himself with the drug and stressed over mistaking his stepdad or John Howard for the government agents. What would either of them do if they found him first and thought he was dead?

He heard scuffling and then saw traces of light from far ahead in the tunnel he turned down. Instantly, he recognized the echoing bellows of his stepdad. "You're not taking me! I'll die first! Do you hear me?" Henry Lee shouted. But then his voice strained as his words sounded muffled. Orrville believed the government agents had finally captured him. He worried they'd take Henry Lee away in the opposite direction, leaving him there in the tunnel.

In a panic, Orrville stretched his hands out, trying to alert the government agents of his presence, searching for something he could make noise with. He felt a metal pipe above his head as he was walking through the darkness. Orrville pulled the syringe from his pocket and stabbed his arm before attempting to make noise rattling it. A burning sensation lasted for a moment as he tossed the syringe away into the darkness, hopefully getting rid of the evidence of his deception. He no longer heard Henry Lee's struggles. Orrville watched the light at the end of the tunnel then began pounding his fist against the metal pipe. For a split second, the light went out. But his continued pounding worked as the light grew brighter and shadows passed through it.

Orrville's body began shaking as his knees gave out, surprised by how quickly the drug's effects were taking hold. Nausea and light-headedness followed with his breathing growing shallow. Wondering if this might be what real death possibly felt like; he turned his head toward the coming light with what strength he had left. Orrville thought they weren't coming for him, as the light grew dimmer. He realized it was his own sight that was failing as he heard the sounds drawing closer. With one final deep breath expelled from his lungs, Orrville blankly stared ahead, succumbing to his false death.

Just before he'd pass out, he heard what sounded like a distant voice utter, "Hey, this is the kid we've been looking for.

Oh man, I think he's dead. His pupils are unresponsive—I don't feel a pulse. No visible wounds. Maybe suffocated. Poor kid. That guy we just caught must have killed him like he killed Fletcher."

Orrville's first reaction to hearing this was to scream out that they were blaming the wrong man for killing his dad. He hoped that the unbalanced John Howard would somehow be punished for his crime. As for Henry Lee, though not a killer, he also deserved to be punished for the things he'd done to him and his mom.

***

Orrville broke free from these thoughts when he heard another man's voice say, "Grab his legs. We need to get him out of here."

"Dump him deep in the woods?" the first man asked.

"Yeah, you know the place. No one will ever find him there."

"Too bad. I bet he was a nice kid."

"Yeah."

Orrville felt the sensation of weightlessness like from a dream. He no longer heard them talking, maybe this was just a hallucination or side effect of the drug. His mind, though, wasn't affected at all, his thoughts clear. Hearing no one will ever find him there worried him, but he remained hopeful and calm, as his dad's plan had worked so far.

So now, all there was to do was wait. Tomorrow the effects of the drug would wear off and he'd find his way out of the woods to escape. Until then Orrville wondered if he could fall asleep and dream. Maybe if the drug did hold some hallucinogenic side effect, he could talk to his mom again. That would be nice.

***

The droning sounds of a woodpecker woke Orrville from the wearing off effects of the drug he'd injected into his body. Snuggling his face closer to something soft, he breathed in a pleasant scent, smelling like wild flowers. Orrville heard what sounded like a wave from the beach his mom took him to when he was ten, competing with the chirping of the birds. He remembered riding next to his mom on a bus all day until they reached the North Carolina Outer Banks to a town called Buxton where they stayed in a small hotel room only a mile from the Cape Hatteras Lighthouse. Walking along the shore with her and building sandcastles was something he wished they could do again.

Rolling onto his back, Orrville opened his eyes, not seeing any traces of ocean, but instead shafts of sunlight piercing the canopy of brilliant colored orange and gold leaves. The sounds similar to ocean waves were made by gusts of wind passing through the branches making the leaves shiver. The autumn foliage reminded him of the beautiful spot in the woods where he'd spread his mom's ashes.

Sitting up, he found himself rather close to the edge of one of the old abandoned coal quarries, overgrown on its edges by the woods trying to reclaim lost ground. Stretching as he looked around, he couldn't think of a more peaceful place to awaken in.

Orrville tried to stand and feeling dizzy, he teetered for a moment on his injured ankle. After taking a step, he fell to his knees. Grabbing his throbbing ankle, he studied the swelling and bruising. He thought it was only a bad sprain and not broken. Reaching out for a fallen branch to use as a walking stick, he made his way out of the woods.

He remembered a man talking about the deep woods and that no one would ever find him here. With a quick gaze around, he found nothing familiar. Considering how remote Birchwood Hollow sat in the Appalachian Mountains, the old notion of finding a needle in a haystack came to mind. If he could just make his way to a road, maybe a driver would be kind enough to pick him up and at least drop him off somewhere close to home.

Orrville pressed on through thick brush and dense trees. Stumbling a few times over jagged twigs and rocks jabbing at his skin, the fallen leaves felt smooth on his bare feet along the path. He recognized the tread marks made by the wheel of a dirt bike left in a dry mud patch. This gave him a sense of hope that the area might not be as remote as the men thought. But this also left him with a couple of lingering questions. He didn't remember spotting any vehicle tracks near where he woke up. So how did his body get there? Did the men walk through the woods, carrying him?

He soon came across a stream of water cascading down a steep cliff. Instead of reaching out his hand to collect water in his palm for a drink, Orrville just stepped fully into the stream. The water felt refreshing, and the taste quenched his dry throat. Orrville returned to the path after he finished drinking. Looking up, he found the position of the sun in the sky shone almost overhead. With luck, he'd find a road before dark if he stayed on the path.

Chapter Ten

"Thanks for the ride," Orrville said to the young driver of a beat-up old black pickup truck.

"Shoot, you're lucky I found you," the guy said. "Promise you won't tell anyone I was up there? I don't want to be thrown in jail for trespassing on government property."

"Your secret's safe, man," Orrville replied with a smile.

"Take care of that ankle," the driver warned. "It doesn't look good."

"I will. Thanks." The driver then pulled away, leaving Orrville at an intersection less than a mile from home.

The bright sunny day had turned cloudy by the time Orrville found the dirt bike rider loading his bike up into the bed of his truck. Orrville hoped he could reach home before the rain fell on him. Rolling claps of thunder and rapid flashes of lightning seemed to challenge this.

Strong gusts of winds clouded the road he walked down with dirt and dust. Branches bent as leaves were wrenched off. Keeping up a steady pace, Orrville reached the mailbox at the end of his long driveway just as the first drops of rain began to fall. By the time he reached his front door he was soaked.

At first he was scared to go inside, but the bellowing thunder and violent flashes of lightning convinced him not to stay outside. Once in his trailer, Orrville looked around. Everything appeared the same as the last time he was home. The only thing missing was Henry Lee, for which he felt happy. Stepping into the small kitchen, he opened the refrigerator door and grabbed the jug of milk, drinking straight from it. Wiping his mouth with the back of his hand, he set the jug on the shelf and took some lunch meat to stave off the hunger pains.

Moving down the hallway, Orrville entered his bedroom. Shedding his soaked jeans, he grabbed a towel and headed for the bathroom for a nice long hot shower. He then returned to his bedroom and dressed in boxer shorts before climbing into bed. Despite the raging storm outside, he pulled his patchwork quilt over his head and within minutes he fell asleep, too exhausted to worry about it.

***

Startled by the high pitch of his alarm clock sounding off, Orrville sat up in bed.

Blinking a few times, he rubbed the sleep from his eyes as his room took focus. Morning sunlight shone through the slightly parted curtains covering his window, revealing dust particles suspended in its beam. Reaching over, Orrville turned off his alarm and looked over at the calendar hanging on his wall. For the first time in days, he truly smiled as he said, "Happy Birthday" to himself. Some might say that eighteen doesn't feel any different from seventeen, but to him it felt exactly as he hoped it would. This was the real beginning of his escape.

Dressing in jeans, a white T-shirt, and a black hoodie, he pulled on his socks and both sneakers. His injured ankle throbbed less than the day before but left him worried that he still might not be able to put weight on it. Testing it when he stood up, he guessed he wouldn't get far without the need for a crutch. As luck would have it, his mom kept a pair of crutches in her closet from when she'd sprained her ankle a year before she died. Orrville found them and took one before heading to the kitchen.

The thought of eating breakfast quickly faded when Orrville found Henry Lee passed out drunk in the old recliner. With his heart in his throat, frighten and confused by how and when his stepdad had been brought back, Orrville wasted no time in returning to his room to quickly pack some extra clothes into his backpack. He also noticed his glasses sitting next to his alarm, having no idea how they'd been returned to him. Henry Lee? He doubted this.

He moved toward the door trying to avoid making any sounds. He stopped when he saw a small pile of money taped to the door near the knob. Grabbing the bills, he forced them into his pocket. He turned the knob and covered his nose as he breathed in the reeking stench of alcohol Henry Lee belched out from across the room.

Once outside, Orrville shifted his eyes around, fearful that he was being watched. Pulling his hood over his head, he used the crutch and hobbled away, disappearing into the woods behind his trailer.

***

Mark Fletcher, soaked and shivering from spending the night out in the storm, spied out from behind the branches of a pine tree. As his heart beat faster, he saw Orrville step outside the trailer and he couldn't help the grin that erupted. His heart sank, though, as he noticed that Orrville was injured. He wanted to rush and help but resisted the urge to. He understood why Orrville appeared nervous and scared. Mark spent years watching Orrville grow into a strong, fine young man through the surveillance cameras hidden in the school and around town. His son was tough and would be okay once he got away from this town.

Wincing in pain, Mark pressed his hand against the bandaged stab wound on his stomach. The blood seeping from it when he was with Orrville in the government testing site had made it appear worse than it actually was. This worked in Mark's favor in helping to deceive him. He had also injected himself with the same drug he'd given Orrville to assist him in finally leaving too. He knew, though, that the government would eventually discover that a vial of the injection drug was missing. And with the understanding of the drug's capabilities, the government would put two and two together and realize their mistake in thinking both he and Orrville had been killed. Would they begin looking for them? Maybe they wouldn't search for Orrville. He hoped they'd leave him alone. But himself, he believed they'd conduct an extensive search in hunting him down. He knew too much and was now a risk to their hidden research.

A part of him felt happy that Orrville wanted them to escape together. But Mark would never have let this happen. That's why he faked his own death. Mark figured Orrville's climb up the air shaft would probably fail. And if Orrville had found him still alive, he wouldn't have chosen the other way out, the one keeping him safe from the government testing.

Mark hoped Orrville found the money he'd left for him after Henry Lee was returned early this morning. He understood the thousand dollars wouldn't last long, but it was enough for him to use in getting away from here. He thought of following him into the woods, watching to make sure he was safe until finding his way out of Birchwood Hollow. But if he did so, he might risk Orrville seeing him. For his son's continued safety he could never let that happen. "I love you. Take care, Son," he mumbled under his breath as he slowly backed away, turning to find his own path from this place.

***

Limping along the side of a winding road leading out of town, Orrville kept anxiously glancing toward the autumn-colored dense tree lines, paranoid, thinking he was being watched. Other than the hoot of an owl and the serenade of a whippoorwill, all was quiet until the distinctive sound from the engine of a long hauler echoed down the road. Hoping the driver would stop for him,

Orrville pulled down his hood and waved as the semi approached and then pulled off on the berm. Balancing on his crutch, he held still, his pulse racing when heard the cab door open and then slam shut.

Orrville couldn't help but smile, overwhelmed with happiness when he saw Zeb appear from around the trailer. He never thought he'd see him again. "Where ya headin', Son?" the old driver asked.

Disheartened to realizing that Zeb didn't seem to remember him, Orrville answered, "As far away from here as I can get, sir."

Walking closer, he looked Orrville firmly in the eye. Winking, Zeb asked, "How does Greensburg, Arkansas sound?" Subtly shifting his eyes, he gave Orrville the impression they were being watched.

"That sounds good, Sir," Orrville answered, attempting to hide his elation that Zeb, in fact, did remember him.

"Well, come on, then. Let me help ya into my truck. We got a long way to go."

"Yes, Sir."

***

A year later

Orrville chuckled as the girl sitting next to him buried her face in his sleeve in fear. As they sat and watched an old space alien evening showing at a drive-in movie theater just outside Lubbock, Texas, he sat back and smiled, looking at Trisha, the pretty waitress he met at a truck stop a few months ago, and thinking about these Hollywood make-believe aliens versus the ones he was led to believe were real. "They won't get you. I'll keep you safe," Orrville whispered in her ear.

Timidly looking up, Trisha smiled at him. "Do you believe in creatures from other planets?" she asked.

Resting his head back on her convertible's passenger seat and gazing up at the stars, Orrville answered, "Maybe. I don't know." Seeing a shooting star, he pointed up, urging her to do so, "Hurry up and make a wish."

Feeling Trisha kiss his cheek, Orrville shyly asked, "Now… what was that for?"

"Well… you said make a wish. That's what I wished for. What about you? What did you wish for?"

Easing her face closer to his, Orrville pressed his lips to hers for a sweet kiss. "That's what I wished for." She beamed upon hearing this.

Orrville noticed the movie's ending credits running on the screen and said, "It's time to go. Could you drop me off at the truck stop?"

"Only if you promise to come here with me next weekend when you're back in town," Trisha insisted.

"Consider it a date," he responded with a grin.

***

Zeb waited in eagerness for Orrville to show up. He rested his back against the trailer and pulled out an old picture of his daughter, Macey, and her son from his pocket. The little boy was adorable, but he never found out his name. Holding it up to the light, he wondered whatever happened to his daughter and grandson. Zeb recalled after she came home from college in Knoxville, Tennessee she revealed she was pregnant. Zeb's wife, Molly, and son, Caleb, were both furious with her. Zeb had urged everyone to remain calm, wanting to hear Macey's side of things. But in the heat of their arguing Macey stormed out of the house and never came back. Though not a churchgoer himself and tolerant of his wife and son's strict Christian faith, he'd reached his breaking point with both of them, scolding them both for how badly they treated Macey. After she left when he wasn't on the road, he tried searching for her near their home in Pensacola, Florida and anywhere around the college in Knoxville. Heartbroken that he failed to find her, Zeb nonetheless held hope that she would return someday.

Months later at Christmastime, Zeb opened a card addressed to him alone, with no return address listed. He knew, though, that it was sent from Tennessee. Inside, he didn't find a card, just a picture of Macey and his grandson. He guessed it was her way of letting him know they were both safe.

Years later after his wife's death and his continued estrangement with his son, Zeb decided to leave Florida to take a driving job in Arkansas. The one advantage was his weekly route through the Appalachian Mountains near Knoxville. In his heart, he knew he wouldn't find her or his grandson, but it helped just passing through that part of the state, feeling a little closer to them each time he drove by.

Zeb noticed a car pull up next to his truck and watched as the pretty driver kissed Orrville before he got out. Waving to her, Orrville turned and walked around the front of the car to the truck. He beamed a smile and pointed at the driver's side door, reading the decal, "*Pike and Son Trucking.* Pa, I can't believe you did that!" Orrville exclaimed as he hugged Zeb.

"Well, the ink on those adoption papers says you're my son. I want everyone else to know too," Zeb responded. "Come on now. We got us a long haul to Santa Fe."

"Yes, Sir."

Later, just inside the New Mexico border, Zeb slowed his truck on a dark lonely stretch of highway when he spotting a stopped car on the side of the road with its lights flashing. Orrville followed him out and walked over to the driver who appeared shaken. "Are ya lost or broken down?" Zeb asked.

The man slowly shook his head, mumbling something Zeb couldn't understand. "Say that again. My ol' ears and hearin' aren't what they used to be."

"*Aliens*," the man mumbled. "There-were-bright-lights-like-I'd-never-seen-before. They-took-me-and-did-things,-experimented-on-me. I'm not lying."

Glancing over at Orrville, they exchanged knowing nods. "Is that so?" Zeb uttered. "Now, don't you worry yourself none. We believe ya."

The man's hands shook as he tried lighting a cigarette. Orrville moved over to help him light it. "What do you think, Pa?" he asked, revealing a slight grin, as he knew what Zeb's answer would be.

"Son, I think this nice man here has himself a real bad case of Harvest Fever."

The End

About Jeffery Martin Botzenhart

You finally made it to the end. I've been eagerly waiting for you. I hope you liked my story. Well then, this is the part where you get to know about me—or as I like to think of it as the part where I bore you. There's really not much to tell. Like Orrville, I grew up in a run-down trailer. But from there in that small Ohio town I graduated from Chalker High School and went on to college at Kent State University. Now, I'm married and have three sons. Other than writing, I enjoy painting and drawing and coach soccer for autistic and special needs kids. But enough about me; let's talk about you. How are you? I see— the silent type. Well, maybe next time. Take care.

Social Media Links:

Facebook:
https://www.facebook.com/jefferymartinbot zenhartwritingjourney/

If you enjoyed this story, check out these other Solstice Publishing books by Jeffery Martin Botzenhart:

Daybreak Nightfall Book One

Amidst a world of cyber surveillance and advancing technology of 2035 San Francisco, Sebastian, a teen runaway, innocently access a sophisticated virtual reality program. The breach of this data proves the catalyst in unraveling corporate and government sanctioned deception of the most unimaginable type. And along with his computer hacker friend, Scotty, both are thrust into a dangerous conspiracy, linking them to a source exposing the truth.

https://bookgoodies.com/a/B073SB9BXG

Painted Desert

Sung with haunting vocals, a spares fragile melody strummed in the dark on a guitar can be one of many disguises for the lonely. Others, either victim of circumstance or of their own devices stay hidden behind colorful masks and pretty decorations to shield their pain. Yet these masquerades hold flaws for hearts searching to heal, revealing not desolate barren souls as any more than a painted desert, but desert angels waiting to lead the lost to the light.

https://bookgoodies.com/a/B072MZY1FK